THE GAME

A H FITZSIMONS

The Game first published 2012
Published in paperback 2014 by CompletelyNovel.com
ISBN 978-1-84914-525-1

Formatting and typesetting: Simon Hartshorne
Printed in the UK

Cover: MICHAL BARAN

For Rebecca

Contents

The Game

I wasn't aware when the switch was tripped. Or how long exactly it took for my mind to accelerate out of control. Maybe as little as a minute. My entire world was spinning, thoughts of the past, present and future, and all possible computations thereof. What if I'd just done this? What if that had just happened? Then I wouldn't be caught in this, then I wouldn't be a…

I'd always hated the word; everything I'd learnt told me to reject it, to banish it from my thinking, but it wouldn't go away. It stomped around in my mind, flaying away in a frenzy of activity. But worse than that, there was the tearing, the awful tearing that began in my solar plexus. The truth was there, the truth was always conceived there and spread outwards like blood seeping through a pure white dressing, a bandage of denial that I had wrapped around it. But now all the purity had gone and I was left with nothing but the truth. And the truth was screaming… Victim. You're a victim. You ARE A VICTIM.

'On a scale of zero to ten, how would you rate your pain, with zero being no pain at all and ten being unbearable?'

They'd asked me that in hospital once. I thought it was a stupid question. How do you measure pain? And what's unbearable pain? If pain was unbearable what would happen? Would you spontaneously combust? No, you would have to bear it. So it wouldn't be unbearable then would it? There's just pain, and how we handle it, how we bear it.

But now I wasn't bearing it. Right now on a scale of zero to ten this was as close to ten as it could get, because I'd had no idea until three hours ago that this level of pain even existed.

For thirty years I had naively been thinking I had my whole life ahead of me. But all I had was what was behind me, and that was a life of one mistake after another. Missed opportunities. Too much time treading water waiting for things to happen. Waiting, instead of living. Holding back waiting for a dream that now would never be. Always holding back.

A sparrow was hopping a few yards away.

Just after my eighth birthday, I remember watching a sparrow being attacked by a mass of other sparrows. I didn't understand what was happening. My mother explained that this was nature; a bird was injured and the others were killing it quickly so that it didn't suffer.

About a month later I'd noticed a baby chick – I couldn't tell if it was a sparrow – lying on its back, naked, bare of feathers, alongside the path in the garden. I wanted to pick it up and protect it, put it in a box with cotton wool and feed it until it regained its strength, until it was better. But then I saw little insects crawling all over its chest, and its tiny eyes showed that pain, the unbearable pain. There was no thought, just my hand reaching out, grasping a big stone and bringing it down hard, driving the chick deep into the ground, so the other birds wouldn't see it, so its pain would stop. I brought the stone down again and again. I wasn't making sure it was dead. I somehow knew I'd killed it with the first blow. I was trying to erase it, bury it deep into the ground and the past. I felt the burning on my cheeks then, and saw the drops of water, suddenly realising I was crying. I didn't know you could cry like that. Silent, scalding tears. My face unmoving, no distortion, no sign of distress. No sign of the unbearable.

As the sparrow flew away I felt those tears again. Where had they been hiding all these years? Right now I was the chick and I needed someone to take a big rock and smash my skull in. End this pain.

That's what I needed but there wasn't anyone; I would have to do it myself.

'Are you alright?'

The voice was so gentle it barely registered. I sat upright and cupped my hands to my eyes.

'Is there any way I can help?'

Slight relief, it was a man's voice, a caring, concerned voice.

I ran my hands downwards over my face, as if to wipe away the torment. The tears were wiped away but nothing else.

He was in his fifties, short blonde hair, his clean-shaven face dominated by thick-rimmed glasses. He reminded me of a boy from school who wore the same type of glasses. Always alone with his books, always top in every exam, he seemed to know everything about everything. I couldn't remember his real name, just that he'd always been called Joe 90, eventually shortened to Joe. Hardly surprising that he was compared with the character in the TV series, the boy who could tap expert knowledge and experience via electrodes hidden in his glasses. It was a standing joke just before an exam started; one of us always asked to borrow those glasses.

What do I tell him?

'Some bad news today,' I say quietly.

There was no sign that he'd even heard me. No banal 'Oh I'm sorry to hear that.' Just a smile, just the warmth in his voice. Just concern.

What to do? It was clear I had to stand up and walk away. I had to do that, what else would I do, tell him? Why not? Why not tell him, a complete stranger, was he not the best person to tell?

'I'm dying… three months, six max.'

No change, nothing.

'My doctor told me the odds of survival are one in a hundred thousand. There's nothing they can do, once you have it, that's it.'

A few moments of silence, what more could I say? It was his turn to speak but he seemed to be content just to sit.

'I should go' I mutter. The silence is unbearable, everything is unbearable.

Finally he speaks…

'What do you fear? It's not the unknown of death is it? In someone as young as you the pain is despair, of lost time, a lost future, lost adventures, a lost life that you probably feel you should have had. And then there's the lost life from the past. A life lived without fully appreciating it. Only when you're dying do you realize how much of life you've let pass you by.'

Words of truth, I know the absolute truth of them, it's been tearing at me for the last three hours. Ripping through me.

'What do you want?'

I watched a seagull float overhead; suddenly I could hear the wind rushing across its wings. I could see inside the clouds above it. I could see everything… and nothing. I had nothing now.

'I don't want to die.'

The words just hung there. How many times have those words been spoken, with the same unbearable pain? Does everyone who realizes the truth that they are going to die say them, does everyone revert back to childhood and make a wish, and just pretend reality isn't there?

'What else?'

What else is there? Get up, walk away.

'Hypothetically, if someone could give you a wish before you die what would you wish for?'

I looked at him, trying to fathom out why he was asking this question. There was no point to this conversation, but there was really no point to anything anymore. So why do anything, why speak, why breathe?

'I want to stop feeling this way, this bad. I want the pain to stop.'

He nods. He understands, but it won't make any difference.

'The pain of your loss, of your lost life. Hypothetically, what do think would erase that?'

'There's nothing.'

'Don't shut yourself off to this because you think it's impossible. Think about it, what *could* erase the pain?'

I wasn't shut off to anything, there was nothing. I knew it, but he wasn't convinced, and a spark of curiosity must have caught fire inside me then. Did he know some secret? Was there something that could stop this tearing in my stomach, stop the voice yelling in my head?

'Tell me.'

'A final adventure, but like nothing you've ever imagined. Daunting, thrilling, an adventure so daring that it will make up for all the missed adventures of the future and provide redemption for all the unappreciated moments of the past.'

I laugh; it's so absurd. Yet I have to hear this.

'Does such a thing exist?'

'It exists, but there's danger with it.'

'I'm dying, how can it be dangerous, what could I possibly lose?'

The wind rustled the leaves on the trees around us. He was looking at the horizon when he spoke.

'Put your affairs in order, and meet me here when you have.'

'What?'

'You've probably not even made any arrangements, no will made out, nothing. Sort it all out; you need to before I tell you what's involved. You need a clear mind.'

I should do that. How long would it take, two, three days?

'Would I meet you here, at this bench?'

'I'll be right here.'

As I left the park, I turned and looked for him. He was still where I'd left him, still looking at the horizon, looking out at the world through those enormous glasses.

*

The promise of something that could end the pain took it down a notch. For the next two days, I spoke to relatives and a lawyer and made funeral arrangements. I went through it all quickly, detached somehow, as if I were making arrangements for someone else.

The promise of what though? It seemed it was my curiosity that was keeping things bearable.

On the morning of the third day I headed for the park. It felt odd as I walked there. It was where I'd first met her. I'd always regarded it as her park. But now it seemed that Joe was encroaching on her territory… he was sitting on her bench.

I sit alongside him.

'Aside from a few signatures next week, everything is sorted, I'm ready.'

'First you must prepare. If I told you today what it was you wouldn't be able to handle it. You wouldn't know how to approach it.'

'I don't understand.'

'Before you set off to climb a mountain you have to go through a lot of preparation. Equipment, food, clothing, planning a route, checking the weather, and also you'd want to be physically prepared, you would have to be in good enough shape to handle the climb, and more, in case anything went wrong.'

'Is that what I'm going to do… climb a mountain?'

'In a sense, but only if you choose to. I can show you where it is, but you will have to decide if you want to climb. You need to prepare, you have to expect problems and know what to use to deal with them. You won't understand right now, but you will when it happens.'

'It?'

'The need to stop. The crushing, overwhelming absolute need to. Where everything you've learned in life screams at you to stop. You must learn how to continue then. You will have to find a way, even though it appears there isn't one. How are you going to do that? How are you going to think outside of your normal responses? What's going to be your driving force?'

'I would find a way because I know this is my final adventure, my last act on earth.'

'That won't be enough. You will have to use things.'

'Use what?'

'Anything and everything. Drop two people into the woods in the middle of a war zone – whilst one will just curl up in a ball frozen by fear, the other will make weapons to fight with. He'll make a bow and arrow. He'll make a knife, a spear, a trap. He'll use what he has, what he can find.'

'I thought this was going to be an adventure, but you're

talking about mountains, war zones, weapons… I'm not following you. And you're not telling me. If I don't know what it is I'm supposed to be doing, how can I know anything… like what weapons to make?'

'You find weapons that allow you to persevere. Weapons that drive you, inspire you, allow you to change, to become someone else… someone who is not limited by preconditioned responses. Someone who will always keep going – when there isn't a reason to, you create one.'

This wasn't helping. I was in the woods, I was in the war zone in my mind and I couldn't see a way out.

'Why can't you just tell me?'

He took a small cloth from his pocket, removed his glasses, and began polishing the giant lenses.

'It's your adventure. It has to not just make sense to you, but mean everything to you.'

I was becoming more confused. *Mean* everything to me. I could feel the tearing starting up again, the truth that this wasn't going to work. Oh, I wanted to believe it would. But there was the underlying question that I hadn't asked, perhaps was too frightened to… how can you make an adventure out of dying?

The hope that he could deliver had been naive. This was crazy. But I was drowning, reaching out for someone to pull me to safety. There was no one else around. What choice did I have?

'Inspiration, motivation, let's call it driving force… where do you think that comes from?'

He was off again, making no sense at all. I was numb. He was waiting for an answer but I didn't have one.

'It's another world for me now, you're asking a question that a few days ago I might have been able to answer, but now I just can't relate to it.'

'There are driving forces so powerful they override the survival instinct. Look at the old warrior cultures; they had no fear of death. The Samurai had a code of honour that overrode everything. The Native Americans believed that they had come from the stars, the furthest reaches of the universe, and when their life was over they would return there, and that they died a good death if fighting for someone they loved. The Spartans took it a stage further and used love: marriage was purely a sexual relationship to produce sons for the Army, the love relationship was between the pairs of warriors, and in battle that pairing always fought side by side. Would you be afraid if you were fighting alongside someone you love? You would be afraid for them, but not yourself. The need to protect is immensely powerful; it was one of the reasons women were taken off front line combat duty in the Israeli Defence Force. The male soldiers started to behave unpredictably when the women they were fighting alongside were wounded or at risk of being captured. The need to protect overrode their training.'

'You're talking about trained soldiers and different cultures, you're talking about rules of war.'

He put his glasses back on, and stood up.

'Haven't you realized? You are at war.'

Perhaps I was after all.

'I'll be here tomorrow, after that you're on your own.'

As I walked home a wave of optimism swept across, catching me, like the lightest breeze at the end of a hot summer's day, before disappearing into the night.

Unable to sleep, I stared out of my bedroom window at a black sky. What was it? What was I missing?

I reach over and lift my wallet from the bedside table, and take from it a photograph. She was the love of my life, and the biggest mistake of my life. I had, in my lethargy for life, taken her for granted. There were too many nights where she had waited up until three in the morning for me to come home. I should have seen what was going to happen... what had I been thinking of? Finally one day she just upped and left. She'd always wanted to travel so it didn't come as a surprise when I received an email from her telling me she was in Barcelona. She said she still loved me but had had enough of living a non-existence. I worried about her. There was a spontaneity, almost a naivety, about her that made her vulnerable; she would do things with little or no regard for the consequences, whereas I just didn't do things. I pondered, I procrastinated. She was so right, I had lived a non-existence. I had wanted her to come back and give me another chance, but what I wanted most, more than anything, was for her to be safe. The pain of my mistake had weighed heavily on me, but now perhaps I could use it. Maybe now my love for her could work for me.

But there was still one fundamental piece of this puzzle missing; one crucial piece had yet to be brought into play. What was I to fight?

Joe knew. I knew he knew, and I knew he would tell me tomorrow.

I hadn't realized it until now, but the pain had gone.

*

'What can I fight?'

'Are you sure you want to? You don't know what's involved.'

'I don't care what's involved.'

'You are preconditioned to reject what I tell you. You will have to overcome everything you've learnt in life. How badly do you want to give everything? Because that's what it's going to take.'

'I've gone through my whole life holding back. I just want one opportunity, one chance.'

'Your doctor said you have a one in a hundred thousand chance of survival.'

'He said it would take a miracle... is that what you want? I'm to fight for that one chance… fight for a miracle? Fight to survive? How do you create a miracle?'

'Miracles, cases of spontaneous healing, often occur with just an act of faith, total faith. Don't become confused when I use the word faith, I'm not talking about religion. Faith is when you truly believe in something that doesn't make any logical sense. You know the absolute truth of it.'

'But you can't know something when reality tells you the opposite.'

'Where is that written? You can fight if you want to, if you choose to. It will be your greatest adventure, fighting to attain an act of total faith. Striving to truly believe you will survive, when there is no logical explanation that you should. Pitting your force of will against logic and reason. Reaching out for the seemingly impossible, changing the entire way you think.'

'And what if I actually reach the point where I truly believe?'

'You may survive; your body might heal itself.'

'I *may* survive, but first I have to accept I *will* survive… a paradox?'

'In a way.'

I couldn't quite grasp that.

'And then there's what you might see as a second paradox.'

I told myself to be ready for this, to open my mind, to use the contradictions.

'This is about death, the most traumatic event of your life, and the way I'm suggesting you deal with it is by turning it into a game.'

'What?'

'A game you played long ago as a child. You had no limits then, no constraints on your imagination. You were free to pretend. Now pretend your body is healing itself and that you're going to survive. That's the way you can truly believe, you pretend something for long enough, it takes over – you start to believe it. Pretend your body is healing itself and that you'll survive, and don't stop pretending.'

'What about the headaches and the other symptoms, how do I keep pretending then?'

'Use them.'

'You think I can use pain, how?'

'Physical pain is a warning signal, the body is telling us that something is wrong. An athlete seeks pain out in training, knowing that only when he continues beyond it will he improve. He sees pain as something that is trying to stop him, but he learns that he can override it. He learns his will is stronger than the pain. When that happens, all the pain is doing is fuelling his self-belief. He learns to love pain.'

'Love something that is hurting us, that we hate… is that the third paradox?'

'You have all the information you need to create the game.'

Too much conflicting information to process, words tumble out… 'So I win the game if I make a miracle, if I survive.'

'There is no winning. There is the game. You play or you don't, it's your choice. Strive towards total faith, play the game according to its rules. If you do this you won't live the way you used to. You won't feel the despair, or the fear, or the loss of life.'

'What will I feel?'

'In charge. In control.'

Control. I liked that word. I wanted to be in control, but

control could only go so far. 'I won't be in control of the headaches…'

'You'll be in control of how you react to the headaches. How you react to everything.'

I caught sight of a group of children playing football at the other end of the park. Cries of excitement reached us. He turned to look at them.

'All I've done is create an outline of the game, the basic principles, the format if you like. But if you choose to play you will have to configure it. It will be *your* game; you have to make the rules, set goals, find ways to discipline yourself and force your mind to think a different way, to persevere. If you can configure the game so that it feels right for you, then you can play it.'

It seemed I was like a child with a toothache to him. He'd come up with a game to stop me thinking about it, a game of distraction. You won't feel the pain of death if you believe you're going to survive. On its own, it was pure denial. But if you take that pretence to the point where you truly believe, and by so doing possibly create a miracle, then you have a purpose to the pretence – you are fighting to survive, and if you're ultimately doing that to protect someone you love, then what started as game of distraction becomes something else entirely.

I had to admit there was a twisted logic to it. But that logic had at its foundation the premise that it was possible to make a miracle happen.

I needed to walk, to be alone. I walked around the park. My mind was dizzy with it all, trying to create order, to find a framework that I could hold onto. I had to make sense of this. I would, if I could find a way around all the paradoxes.

When I returned to the bench it was empty.

I wasn't surprised. I somehow knew I would never see him again, and that now I should take his basic principles and make something out of them. But I felt it acutely, the solitude, the sense of loss, the sheer enormity of what faced me.

An hour later I was back in my flat when I realized the game couldn't work… and the switch was tripped.

Was it possible to make so many mistakes? Why so many? If I hadn't made the mistake with her, everything might have worked out, I could have had a life worth living… I could have lived. I am thirty and I am totally alone. This is how I am going to end my life.

Perhaps she wasn't a mistake after all. Perhaps I would have ruined her life as well.

I didn't think that though. I didn't believe it. She would have inspired me to do something, if only I'd given her the chance.

What if? I'd said it so often in my life, but now it seemed my life had swung on decisions made in split seconds. The weight of those seconds was stifling, suffocating… no, that wasn't it; it was heartbreaking.

Now I understood why people die of a broken heart. And die so quickly.

I thought of the game, it was still there. But it would just allow the despair, the heartache, to last longer.

You're too frightened to play it.

Don't start those tactics.

One last chance at redemption?

Redemption doesn't mean anything to me just now. I am caught in a world of self-pity. I pity myself for making all those mistakes. Now I have to pay for those mistakes.

Perhaps the game is your penance.

I can't play the game, because I have to believe, in the game, and in myself, in order to play it.

The belief will come as you play.

No matter what I do, the mistakes aren't going to go away. I see them clearly now. There will be no redemption.

You can at least try. You owe it to yourself, for one day, just try it. See it as a single day, and only one day.

I reasoned I could do that.

Tomorrow then.

As I lie in bed, I think of how it will be tomorrow. I don't want there to be any reason to go back to the game after that. If I was going to play for a day, then I would give everything to that day.

It will be my last act.

*

For the first few hours it felt like I was trying to swim, but against the current in a shark-infested ocean. What I was doing was incredibly wrong on every level.

Just today. Just this hour. Just this minute, I would tell myself, and the minutes stretched into eternity.

I had set the target of midnight, and I was going to see it through. It wasn't to see what would happen. I was certain it wouldn't work, pretence wouldn't take over, I wouldn't start to believe. But the fact remained I didn't know, because I had never tried, I had never once committed myself totally to an act of faith for any length of time. This was the one thing I had left to do before I died. Prove that Joe was wrong, prove that his idea for a game was stupid.

Just this hour, just this minute, and for each minute I ignored the sharks and kept pushing out against the current, into the unknown.

It was the most testing, and longest, day of my life, but in the evening something odd happened, a trace of optimism found its way into my thoughts. Perhaps because there was no let-up to my pretence, I began to feel it might work. I began to believe I might survive.

By midnight I believed. For one day, I had deceived myself.

I was exhausted, but euphoric. It was a cloudless sky, one of those nights I used to take for granted. But tonight I walked for hours under the umbrella of the stars. And I saw, in the stillness of the night, that the game was giving me the chance to free my mind. I stared upwards and saw where the game could take me. Beyond the rules of the way I'd thought my entire life. Into the unknown.

What lay out there? What would happen if, against logic and reason, I truly believed?

As for the chances of survival, that really would take a

miracle. Was it just a suicide mission? Like the one given to the dozen soldiers in World War Two who were on death row – one last chance to clear their Army records and die fighting the enemy. *The Dirty Dozen* may have been a fictional film, but I was sure it had its roots in reality, and I could remember, when I watched it, wondering why some of the soldiers took so long to make their decision. I had thought if I were in their position I would jump at the chance; would it not be better to die fighting than passively? Would it not be better just to do something? To exert a level of control over death?

And I wanted to be in control.

Was it the ultimate test of will, the ultimate challenge, the ultimate risk? Or the ultimate fantasy? The ultimate act of stupidity? Reaching out for something that was beyond reach – and if somehow I did reach it, would it change anything? Do miracles happen when you truly believe?

The sky shows signs of lightening by the time I arrive home. I cross the living room to the wall next to the kitchen, where I write the number one. Day One of the game. I need to have a record. I need to look at each day as a separate war.

*

Day Two I started on the defensive; I kept my dream of recovery protected behind a wall with reality on the other side. After an hour, doubt began to find its way through. At first I barely noticed it, then little things, things relating to my situation, established themselves. Then the wall began to crumble. I managed to shut out despair, but I saw clearly that yesterday was a one off. It worked only because it was supposed to be for one day. I never imagined I would play for longer.

I wasn't ready. I needed a structure to adhere to, rules I had to follow. I need a basic control mechanism.

I lay in bed thinking about it, eventually deciding that going on the defensive was the wrong thing to do. I had nothing to gain, just something to lose. I went through different options until I came up with something. It was childish, it would be laborious, but it was a starting point, and it might work. It was an idea stolen from a computer game where you had three lives; if you lost one, or two, you could replenish life, represented by a small red heart, by achieving some goal on screen.

I would start each day with ten lives, ten red hearts. If I lost them all I would lose the game for that day. I would lose a life if I thought of death, or became depressed or afraid. I would gain a life if I successfully pretended I was going to survive for a period of time, or if I believed for even a few minutes. If I reached twenty lives, the next stage was blue hearts. I would aim to get into the blue zone, and finish there, every day.

*

Day Three and I find out very quickly how little control I have over my thoughts. I lose all my lives by early afternoon. The next day it's the same. The blue range was fantasy.

The fifth day I lose all ten by mid-morning.

At first I didn't understand. I was certain I was picking up on my negative train of thought more quickly. Then I realized I was beginning to exert a level of control, yet I was penalising myself for doing so.

I readjusted. The rule was that if I identified negative thoughts within a minute or so of their onset, and then corrected myself, I would not lose a life. As I become more adept I would reduce the time allowed.

But that didn't happen. I kept losing lives. I couldn't keep it going; the level of concentration required was impractical. Often I would go from hour to hour forgetting what I was supposed to be doing, or how many lives I had left.

By Day Ten it seemed hopeless. The only time I was not losing lives was when I became caught up in a task, where my mind was totally occupied. I realized I should have targets, an example of belief in the future that I could try to replicate. I needed to identify some imagery that I would associate with recovery. What though? Meeting her in the park a year from now? It was an absurd picture, an impossible future, but it was an image, and it became a series of images that I could visualize. Receiving an email saying she was back and wanted to see me, getting ready to go out to meet her. Walking to the park past the completed blocks of flats that they'd barely started working on. From those images short films branched off, all of them associated with being alive, one year from now.

*

Day Twelve started badly. I had my images, my films from the future, but instead of playing them out, I was arguing…

You just can't make miracles happen. What you're trying to do makes no sense.

I'm dying, things don't have to make sense anymore. I can do whatever I want.

In that moment, I saw clearly that it didn't have to make sense, nothing had to. If there was ever a time I could do whatever I wanted, it would be now. But that didn't seem to matter, the logic of the game: the honourable death, the great adventure, the suicide mission, fighting for a miracle. They were all a jumble of words, because right now they meant nothing. What mattered was what I felt. And now I felt deep depression.

I felt this way every time I pretended, started to believe, and then crashed back to reality.

Use the depression, don't look for a different path, become more determined. Instead of responding as you would normally, by lowering your goals, make them higher. Be more committed in your levels of pretence and belief; you will know you're succeeding if your depression is deeper.

I knew that was Joe talking. He thought you could apply the rules of war to everything.

There was just too much conflict.

You need to start finding weapons, things to use.

Men who use weapons have been conditioned to die in combat. I'm not conditioned for anything.

You don't have to be. Would a mother, or father, not feel

they had a good death if they died protecting their children? Would they fear death? It's about having a reason, a cause worth dying for.

*

Sitting on the bench I take her picture from my wallet. An hour later I visit a PhotoShop and have the picture copied, then order it to be made into poster size. It will take a few days before it's ready but I will hang it on the wall across from my bed. I will look at her face when I need to be reminded why I play the game, when the headaches are bad.

It's an act that lifts me, drives me for the next few hours but now I'm thinking of her… missing her. This is not helping. This is destructive. If I were going to see her again I would be dreaming of just that, not thinking of the past. But that's all I can think of. The memory of her still sends a charge of electricity through me.

This was supposed to be about protecting her, but she's a thousand miles away. Then what was it about? It was about me, my desire, my need to change things so that I would be well, and with her now.

If the game was going to work this had to be about love; if I could smother desire then I could use the need to protect. She may be far away now, but there may come a point in the future when she needs me. Who knows what will happen? We still exchange the occasional email, there's still that fragile line of contact. She knows I would be there for her if ever she needed me. It didn't matter how unlikely it was. It *might* happen. The only way I can protect her is if I am alive. The game gives me a chance to stay alive.

There was honour there. I had had to dig deep to uncover it but it was there. The game, at this stage, seemed dependent on my smothering desire.

How do you do that? How do you switch off from something so powerful?

*

I wake to darkness, I hear the voice clearly. I know that voice. Death is calling me, It's at the door of my bedroom and it's the most awful voice I've ever heard, it penetrates my soul and I am like a child, terrified. I first heard it the night I was told the news...

All that night it had kept me awake, wondering if Death had manifested itself into intruders in my flat. I lay awake listening for the slightest sound. But what could I do if Death had taken a physical form? I was being thrown back into my childhood.

When I woke from a nightmare, my imagination ran amok. Something evil was outside my bedroom and nothing my mother did could console me. I would not stop screaming. When my father returned home that Friday evening he came into my room carrying a parcel. A present, but one unlike any other. 'This is not a toy,' my father whispered. I unwrapped it carefully. A sword? 'Not just any sword. A sword made in a faraway place, a secret place; it is called a Scimitar.' My father went on to tell me how feared this sword was, that it had only to be drawn to send enemies into flight. He described great battles which had raged on with no end in sight until a regiment of horsemen, cavalry, had arrived armed with Scimitars. With their appearance on the field of battle, their Scimitars catching the sunlight, the enemy instantly threw down their weapons and surrendered. Then he made me promise not to take the sword outside my bedroom, to keep it safe, to guard it, as it would guard me. He didn't mention the nightmares, but they never troubled me after that night, that magical night.

Ten years later we moved house. My mother, in her need to transport as little as possible, threw out everything deemed as not essential; the wooden sword disappeared at that time. I no longer needed it.

But times change, and not long after the game started I went online looking for a steel version, for a real Scimitar. I didn't find one, but I found something as good, as it was the same shape, and proportionately, for an adult, the same size. And like in my childhood I would keep the same promise I made to my father: I would never take it out of the bedroom. I couldn't, it was so obviously lethal, if I had ever ventured outside carrying it I would have been arrested within minutes...

It's not a reflex action; I have to think about it. My fingers struggle to move at first, then, inch by inch, my hand slides tentatively down the bed. The fear starts to dissipate the moment my fingers fold around the handle of the machete. At that moment I feel a level of control. Because it will protect me against any intruders, physical or from my dream world. The machete doesn't care which, it will allow me to fight whatever I have to, including the voice of death. The machete is a weapon, it is a symbol of the game. It allows me to banish the voice quickly. It is a reminder that I am not a victim, that I am in control.

I tell myself that. I tell myself that if I say it often enough, I will start to believe it.

*

By Day Thirty I had added more elements to the game, things that I know are good for the immune system – laughter, and feelings of love and compassion. I had made a short DVD of scenes from films that brought on these positive emotions. I had watched the DVD so often, sometimes I would close my eyes and just lie back and listen to the words and let my imagination play out the images. I would score a life every time I played the DVD. I sought out inspirational films and watched them. I was trying to create a world where miracles were everyday occurrences, where medical science was repeatedly being challenged and proved to be flawed.

I was tuning into my thoughts and emotions far more than before. The game itself was becoming more structured. There were more rules, more goals, more incentives, and there was more conflict. And when I wasn't pretending, when reality hit me, more depression.

Respite was brief, just before I fell off to sleep. Then I would see myself in a small space ship flying out of the solar system and through distant galaxies. I was free of conflict, my body and mind suspended in the weightless state. Out there I was free of everything. I roamed in uncharted areas of the universe and imagined that I was tapping an immense power. A power that was unimaginable on Earth, a power logic would always fail to measure as there was nothing about it that humans could understand. I didn't try to understand it. I just accepted it. The only thing I knew about it was that you had to be out there, out in the furthest reaches of the universe, to be able to tap it.

After my first flight into space I wondered about the spaceship, and decided that on my next flight I would look at it from a distance, to see what had allowed me to travel so far. It was small, only a few feet long, made of hard metal, shaped like a half avocado cut horizontally, the cockpit where the stone had been. There was no glass or protective covering for the cockpit. I just sat upright, holding on to the steering wheel. And it was royal blue. It was the colour that gave it away. How often I insisted to my parents that I went on the blue one, stubbornly refusing to go on any of the red, yellow, or green spaceships at the fair. I should have known: only the spaceship of my childhood would allow me to travel so far into deep space.

I was retracing flight-paths I'd made twenty-five years earlier. I was seeing the universe through the eyes of a five-year-old.

*

My teeth are chattering, my whole body is shivering as I step out of the bath. I grab the towel and wrap it around me. I hate the cold baths. Even though they only last for a couple of minutes, I hate them with a passion. Too often I wake and just feel the longing for her, the softness of her alongside me, her arm wrapped around my chest, the smell of her hair. I have learnt to use things with the game but desire is a like a dark shadow that makes me question the extent of my love. My desire for her is selfish. From it branches jealousy. The game cannot be about self, the game must be about her. I cannot play the game, and reach out into the unknown, if I am concerned about myself.

But it's difficult. I still want her. My desire for her remains out of my control. Although I hate the cold baths I take comfort in the belief that if I can control desire, I can control anything.

*

I wake and my mind is a mess. Reality is pressing down on me.

Nothing is working. I have fought through forty-eight days of the game, but I can't see a way through the conflict today.

Do you want to end it?

Do you want to accept death and put an end to the game, or do you want to stay with the suicide mission for another day?

I either played or didn't play. I wanted a clear choice every time I began to doubt. Posing the question broke my train of thought, shoving the choice slap-bang in my face, preventing reality from sweeping through me. It was a throwback to a time of innocence before the silent tears, when my best friend would run the fifteen yards from his house to mine, and call out to me, a time when every day was an adventure. This may be a war game, that thrived off conflict, but it was still a game; it was based on pretence.

I will play the game today, but each day is more difficult than the one before. I was pretending, but to truly believe, I had to have total faith, and that meant I had to know. And knowing was a feeling, you could not force a feeling. You could only encourage it. Make the conditions more conducive to it happening.

And right then I had a feeling that I was no longer encouraging it. Deep down I was tired, not just of the conflict, but of the search for things to use, then finding they would only work for a few days – the search was almost constant. The truth of the reality that I was going to die was set in stone. I was attempting to break that stone and replace it with an opposing truth – that I was going to survive. But my pretence was like waves that constantly broke their backs against the stone. And whilst the stone of truth, of death, remained intact, I wilted.

The only time I had really challenged actual reality was when I escaped from it, in my blue spaceship. It was as if I could not fight it on its terms. I could not break the stone of truth, not with something from this world. It seemed I would have to travel to a place far away to find a weapon that could break it. But there had been so few successful flights, the last one having been over ten days ago.

The child in me lay silent.

I was running out of ideas. I was running out of time.

*

Day Fifty-Five of the game, and the sun was shining through the curtains. It was summer, and with the memory of changing seasons and my joy at this time of year, came reality. I felt the emptiness in my stomach. I felt the loss of life. It was a cruel reality to have to acknowledge that there was no future, there was nothing, that my whole existence now amounted to a childish and stupid game.

For fifty-four days I had been trying to block out reality. But this morning the feeling of loss was overwhelming. I had no children, no legacy, no wife, nothing… except a game. I felt it this time, the switch being tripped, the tearing starting up in my stomach, the screaming…

Despair and emptiness, and a life of mistakes. I throw back the covers and stumble through to the kitchen. A minute later I'm lying back in bed, looking up at the knife. I feel in control, I have a choice – the game or the knife. That was what my thirty years on Earth now amounted to.

I had read that the quickest way was to slide it directly into the heart between the fifth and sixth ribs. With my right hand I count upwards until I find the right spot. I sit up on my knees, about to lean forwards, but the knife is too far away. I grab the bedside table and position it on the bed, holding on firmly to the knife handle with both hands and keeping it fixed at an angle at the edge of the table. I lean forwards until the point of it touches my skin. If I kick my legs backward, my body will drop forwards and the knife should slide in easily. A handful of seconds. That's all. One for each of my most terrible mistakes.

The point of the knife is sharp. I feel it break the skin and watch a drop of blood trickle down the blade. Too easy, far too easy to end it this way, when you've still your greatest weapon left unused.

I can't do that.

What makes you think you ever had a choice?

I roll backwards and fall over onto my side. I feel like a tree crashing to the ground, its last act the slow, inevitable fall to earth. And I lie there, letting the trauma wash over me. My hands start trembling, my whole body is shaking.

I want a way out, but all I can see is the mountain. A mountain to climb now. I'm at the foot of it, looking up, and I'm worn out.

Find a way. Make a start, one step. Do it, *now*.

My fingers open, releasing the knife. I haul myself out of bed, throw on some clothes, and go online. I buy a number of things to use. Posters of my favourite films to cover the walls, and one to cover her picture – I can't bring myself to take her picture down, but there was nothing to be gained in fuelling desire. Ice cube trays; the baths need to be colder. I send off emails severing the last ties I have to society, to normality. I will live in isolation. I will not think about this morning again.

I wrap the knife in paper, bag it, and later drop it into a street bin.

A new phase of the game begins.

*

It's midnight, the wind is rattling the bedroom windows.

I sit on the side of the bed and run water over the whetstone, then run the blade of the machete down it. I like the sound it makes. The sound of steel caressing stone, the roughness then the light ringing as the blade leaves the stone. I like the feel of it, there is something addictive to it, just running steel against stone. Is it something primeval, or the association with images from the past? Not the butcher's fast five second sharpening, this was deliberately slow. And I'd seen it numerous times in war films. The night before battle, soldiers would spend so much time sharpening their swords or knifes. I used to wonder why so long, when the blade must have been sharp anyway. Now I knew: it was peaceful, calming, and they were making a statement – tomorrow horrors are going to happen, and they may die, but do their hands tremble? No, because they are in control; their resolve is at one with the steel.

Mine isn't, but I will continue to pretend it is.

*

I walk slowly towards the bench. From the storm last night branches lie all over the park, like Godzilla had been through swiping at the trees.

I sit and run my fingers through my hair, over my childhood, over my adult life, over almost two hundred days of the game. And those days somehow seem very separate from the rest of my life. How much the game has changed me.

Should I have played it? Had the game ever given me a choice? It had seduced me into playing it. It made all these promises. Play me, it entreated, play me and I'll take away the pain, I'll give you the greatest adventure, a chance to survive, and if you die I'll give you an honourable death fighting for someone you love… play me and you won't be a victim.

But as soon as I'd started there was no more gentle persuasion, the game was all about coercion. When I'd used everything yet still struggled, I had no choice but to turn to the rules of war. And doing so gave me not so much a reason to play, but an immensely powerful reason to not stop playing. From that point the game had become very simple, essentially a hybrid of two warrior codes, the Samurai and the Spartans, a mercenary marriage of the most potent aspects of both, which used the best weapon I had. It was then that the cold, calculating side of the game came to the fore, making me feel that I would be betraying her if I didn't keep playing. It exploited love and it exploited shame.

Day Sixty seemed a lifetime ago, but by the time I passed it, the rules of the game were so strict that they made everything black and white: I played, pretended, or I didn't play.

I fought to protect her by pretending, or I accepted reality and betrayed her. By Day Eighty everything had become symbolised with imagery: the beauty of her smile as she walked towards me in the park with the completed flats in the background, against my turning my back on her and walking away when she desperately needed my help. There was never a middle ground. Every single time I doubted, or questioned, or hesitated, or wilted, I had to make exactly the same choice: play or betray? Always I chose to play. I chose to pretend and protect her – pretend and defend. Put that way, did I have a choice? It was more than habitual; I conditioned myself not just to see the images unfold with the two separate decisions but to feel acute shame with one and honour with the other. The repeated use of the two phrases eventually negated the need to consciously play out the images. 'Play or Betray?' and the answer 'Pretend and Defend' became trigger phrases that short-circuited my natural thought process. They didn't just stop me from thinking that I was going to die, they effectively forced me into pretending I was going to survive. I longed for a time of peace, but I had become a prisoner of the game, of a twisted love, a love that drives you because it makes you ashamed of betraying the subject of that love.

I have distorted love and used shame to find a way to maintain pretence and believe. But all my senses still tell me not to believe. It seems I will always be at war with a lifetime of conditioning, against everything I know, and feel.

I would continue to play, but in one hundred and ninety days was I any closer to truly believing? The stone of truth, that I was going to die, remained solid and fixed. It was below the surface, deep in my subconscious, and it affected everything. It formed the foundations of the way I thought, the way everyone thought. It formed the basis of logic.

I stand and begin the walk back to the flat. I have to walk around Godzilla's victims. Victim, that was how it all started. The thought that I was one had triggered the tears.

If I could go back and replay it would I change things? Although the creation of the rules had been trial and error, the game itself was a trial. But more importantly, somewhere in all those days I had lost my identity. As if, through the game, I had mutated into a machine, a computer that had a programmed response for everything… and used the woman I was supposed to love.

A soulless robot.

I missed life. I missed living.

I stopped in my tracks and looked down at a broken branch.

Why are you doing this, or is this the game's doing?

The need to take control, finding things to use, pain, weapons, turning everything into a fight. But there was also the need to revert back to my childhood: the machete with its link to the magical sword, the poster size picture of her, the same way I had idolised film stars, the escapes in the blue spaceship, the game itself, and the games within the game… all that pretence. I kept trying to enter the world of my childhood but I was constantly being blocked by the desire of an adult. She was my greatest weapon, but also the source of my greatest conflict, that even ice cold baths failed to control. That desire kept me and my spaceship grounded in reality, in the world of logic. So I resorted to more unforgiving methods to take control and reach out for a miracle, that culminated in the Samurai Spartan hybrid. But why? Why had I gone to such extremes?

I was so caught up in the game I had lost track of what it was about: despair, the despair of dying a victim, a victim of my mistakes; the pain of that was unbearable. When I was eight, I'd felt unbearable pain seeing the dying chick, and I had been shocked at the brutal way I had erased that pain. The tears, the silent scalding tears, had transformed me back into that ruthless child, who had at first played a game to create the game, using Joe. Then, having served his purpose, Joe was thrown into a cupboard like an unwanted toy, as the child began to turn the game into something cruel and ugly. I was blinded to what was really going on, to the mercenary side of it, because I had programmed myself to believe that the game was noble – all about protecting her – but in fact it was all about me. The game, from Day One, had been protecting me.

And I was sick of me. I had had enough of manipulating, using emotions… using her. I wanted to feel love. I yearned to express my love for her, and through her, my love for life.

Then stop using her as a weapon. End the game. Accept death and face the loss and the despair. Die as a man; don't fight through each day as a machine.

I will die loving her.

I walk back to the flat and I can feel it, spreading out from my solar plexus. I needed to know that there was love for her, that some trace of my humanity was left intact. But somehow the truth of it is more than a counter balance against the illiberal, mercenary side of me, and the game I had created – it is like a protective shield.

I see the perfect way to express that love before I died.

By playing a different game, as a man who has accepted death. By continuing with the pretence, purely as an act of love.

At the flat, I tear down the film poster that covers her picture. I no longer feel desire; it was as if my desire for her had been inexorably linked to my desire for life. No wonder it had burned so furiously until now.

That night I leave the curtains open. As I lie in bed looking up at the stars I realize there is no longer anything written in stone, no rules, no fear of despair, no fear of anything. I am free to pretend, indifferent to what might happen. And I see that the paradoxes, like planets, have finally fallen into alignment and that what I am doing now might actually produce a miracle. But whether it does or doesn't no longer matters. I just wonder what has brought about this sudden change. Is it because I have given everything to the game? Victims don't fight back; was it the sheer severity and duration of the conflict that had allowed me to feel I had finally given everything to life? Or was it that I have reached the goal I'd set myself – to accept I was going to survive – and it was irrelevant that, in order to do so, I'd had to accept I was already dead? Had I found peace in the ultimate paradox?

I knew what it was: I no longer cared what happened, because 'I' ceased to exist at the precise moment I was willing to stop playing the game, so that I could die loving her.

I look across at the wall, and in the moonlight I can just see the outline of her face in the picture, yet I've always seen clearly every curve and line of that face. Every time I buckled over in pain, every time I caught sight of myself in a mirror and saw a gaunt stranger looking back, every time I lay shivering or threw up a mix of bile and blood, every time the trauma was so bad that there wasn't time to think of trigger phrases or pretending, and I wanted to just end it all, I saw her face, willing me on. I hadn't realized it until now, because I had denied all of those moments as soon as they were over. I had fought through each day then crossed it off the following morning as if it hadn't happened. And to think I had questioned my love for her. When reality was at its worst, it wasn't the game that protected me, it was that love. I had been manipulating and distorting everything so I could play the game, but I had loved her from the beginning. She had always been the cause worth fighting for, and the cause worth dying for.

I look out again at the moon and the stars beyond it; infinity lies out there, waiting for me. I feel the engines of my blue spaceship fire up. Tonight I will travel a billion light years per second. Tonight my love for her will light up the darkest regions of the universe.

Anton FitzSimons began writing following a sixteen month stay in hospital due to advanced lymphoma. He was less than half his normal bodyweight after undergoing a series of operations, including the removal of two major organs. A 'do not resuscitate' order was given following a brain stem stroke. Shortly afterwards, treatment for the lymphoma was found to be ineffective, his consultant later stating that at this point survival was deemed impossible. The sister in charge of the high dependency unit, where he spent five of his ten months in isolation, described his recovery as a miracle.

Throughout this entire period he played a version of the game described in this story.

www.extrememental combat.com

www.ingramcontent.com/pod-product-compliance
Lightning Source LLC
Chambersburg PA
CBHW070454170726
48291CB00005B/1752